ABOUT THE AUTHOR

Adeeba Jafri is a Pakistani-American writer, teacher and IB Coordinator from NY, currently based in Doha, Qatar. A graduate of Barnard College, Columbia University, she has authored multiple children's books: *The Baby Garden, The Path that Allah Made, Alia and the Story of the Rose* and *A Zoom with a View.* Her writings have been featured in various blogs and literary journals, including BluntMoms, YourTeenMag, Fahmidan Journal, The B'K magazine, Raising Mothers, Prohze, Agapanthus Collective, and Poetically Yours.

Show Yourself is her first collection of YA novellas.

SHOW YOURSELF

SHOW YOURSELF

ADEEBA JAFRI

Cherish
EDITIONS

First published in Great Britain 2021 by Cherish Editions
Cherish Editions is a trading style of Shaw Callaghan Ltd & Shaw
Callaghan 23
USA, INC.
The Foundation Centre
Navigation House, 48 Millgate, Newark
Nottinghamshire NG24 4TS UK
www.triggerhub.org

British Library Cataloguing in Publication Data A CIP catalogue
record for this book is available upon request from the British Library
ISBN: 978-1-913615-19-2
This book is also available in the following eBook formats:
ePUB: 978-1-913615-20-8
Adeeba Jafri has asserted her right under the Copyright,
Design and Patents Act 1988 to be identified as the author of this work
Cover design by More Visual
Typeset by Lapiz Digital Services

To my parents, Aziz and Zakirun Jafri

FOREWORD

As a writer, a speaker, someone with clinical depression, and an advocate for normalizing mental health conversations, I am thrilled to write the foreword for Adeeba's book, which addresses the subject with great sensitivity. Just like we don't feel ashamed to talk about diseases of the human body – like diabetes or cancer – we shouldn't hesitate to talk about mental health issues, which are nothing but a malfunctioning of the human brain, just like any other disease.

Not only is *Show Yourself* a gripping novel that makes you want to read the entire book in one sitting, but it also tackles the sensitive topic of mental health among children and young adults in a very subtle way. It is unfortunate that in some conservative communities, talking about mental health is still considered a taboo subject, with issues often shrugged off as a phase that will pass on its own. The signs indicating underlying mental health issues are often misinterpreted and misconstrued as a lack of faith or spiritual connection. Adeeba handles the subject very intricately and highlights the importance of identifying & recognizing those signs as the first step towards helping someone who may be suffering alone in silence.

The book revolves around the lives of three teenage girls in a Muslim community based in North America. The book highlights the challenges faced by a typical teenager today, as their lives revolve around academia friendships, sibling rivalries, and devices. As she weaves an exciting plot around the teenage relationships, she also taps into the complexities of teen relationships and opens the floor for conversation around mental health issues in kids. This book is a conversation starter about mental health and as such, it's a step in the right direction – an excellent read for all.

Shehar Bano Rizvi
Storyteller | Photographer
www.diaryofapmpmom.com

CONTENTS

GLOSSARY

Assalaamu Alaikum - a proper greeting among Muslims that translates to "peace be with you"

Asr – one of the five daily prayers for Muslims

Baji – Urdu / Hindi term of endearment for an older sister

Duas – invocations to God, usually made after prayer

Halaqa – discussion circles among Muslims

Hijab – traditional headscarf worn by Muslim girls / women

Insh'Allah – an Arabic term that translates to "God willing"

Karak chai – black tea brewed with cardamom and condensed milk

Kurta – shirts customary of Southeast Asian culture

Masjid /mosque - place of congregation and prayer for Muslims

Qur'an – the holy book for Muslims

Salaam – shorthand for '*Assalaamu alaikum.* Literally means "peace" in Arabic

Wa alaikum as-Salaam – a proper response to the greeting '*Assalaamu alaikum*'

Wudhu – ritual cleansing done prior to daily prayer

CHAPTER 1

THE THREE FRIENDS

"Is anyone listening? Hellooo?"

With monumental effort, Lena plucked her AirPod out of her ear to meet her mother's glare in the rearview mirror.

"Girls," continued Lena's mother, Salma, tight-lipped and clearly irritated, "can you please message Hana and say that we're parked and waiting outside the house?" She stared at the digital clock in the centre of the car's dashboard, feeling more anxious as every second passed. This was an everyday occurrence. Today, however, Salma was in even more of a mood, and it was mainly to do with the girls being distracted by their phones.

"Aliya was just showing me a video, Mama, but we're done now," Lena said, looking pointedly at her childhood friend, who was seated next to her. Aliya begrudgingly followed suit and put her phone away. However, she left the AirPods – a recent gift for her 14th birthday – in her ears, then pulled her black hoodie over her head, leaned back and closed her eyes, content in her world of music.

"What's taking so long? We're going to be late!" yelled Lena's ten-year-old brother, Ali, from the backseat. Despite having to jostle between Lena's basketball and Aliya's lacrosse stick, Ali always sat in the back of Salma's four-by-four rather than taking the empty space in the middle row. "I'm not sitting with Lena Baji's friends. They smell," was his usual pronouncement.

"They're coming out now," said Salma, phone in hand, having resorted to texting Fatima herself.

Before long, the car door opened and Hana slid in next to Aliya and Lena with her characteristic grace – a feat, considering how low the car's ceiling was. Hana was taller than the other two girls by at least two inches.

"Salaam, everyone! Sara will be out in a minute, Salma. She's just getting her ice skates."

Sara, an eighth grader at the same school, was a year younger than the girls. She had been taking ice-skating lessons since she was five. Lena had never had the chance to see her on the rink, but Hana mentioned that she had vastly improved since starting.

"Salaam, dear. No worries." As Sara approached the car, Salma reached over to open the door. "You can sit in the front today, Sara. The girls were watching something together in the back, but *now* they've put their phones *away*." There was definite force to some of her words.

Sara, petite and quiet as always, put her bag and ice-skating equipment into the car. She was bundled up in a long-sleeved shirt and jacket despite the heat. Even the short walk from the front door to the car had left her sweating profusely.

That's a lot of layers, Lena thought. Her mother must have been thinking the same thing because Salma said, "Sara, aren't you a bit layered up for this weather?"

Sara smiled and replied, "I go straight to the rink after school and it gets pretty cold on the ice."

Salma nodded as she pulled out of the brick-paved, circular driveway, characteristic of the beautiful homes that lined Hana and Sara's street.

On the way to school, Lena, Hana and Aliya prattled on about their recent Netflix binge while Salma asked Sara some polite questions about ice skating, though it sounded more like an interrogation. Ali immediately sensed his mother's intent and yelled from the backseat, "You're not putting me in any ice-skating class, so don't even think about it!"

There was no time to respond because, just then, Salma pulled into the carpool lane at Hamza Academy and all five kids shuffled out. Ali practically jumped out of the trunk and bolted off with a "See you at 3pm! Salaam!"

As the girls entered the school and walked towards their lockers, Hana pulled Lena and Aliya aside. "Come to my house after school," she said, conspiratorially. "I want to show you guys something."

"What is it?" Lena asked, but Hana was already walking away, a smile on her face.

"You know how it is with her and hobbies. She's probably signed up for ballet classes to compete with her sister's ice-skating lessons," said Aliya, in a bored voice.

Aliya took her AirPods out and started tapping on her phone in a frustrated manner, muttering "Why… won't… you… connect?" As she tapped, Dr. Shaukat, the grumpy English teacher walked by, looking directly at her and Lena.

Knowing that phones weren't allowed in school, Lena gave Aliya a quick nudge to get her attention. Aliya looked up and practically threw the phone into her bag, saying, "Uh, I'll see you later."

Lena shrugged and headed to her homeroom class, wondering about Hana's surprise.

CHAPTER 2

NO SURPRISE

On the ride home, Hana sat in the front with her mother while Aliya and Lena pestered her about her secret. The car ride was calm, given Ali's absence. He had stayed after school for robotics, though Lena imagined he spent more time destroying the robots than putting them together. Sara, meanwhile, was at the ice rink.

As soon as Hana's mom pulled onto the driveway, the girls jumped out and followed Hana to her room, carefully dodging the minefield of intricate and expensive decorations that were scattered throughout the house. What Lena loved about Hana was that even though her family was clearly in a very different position, she never let Lena or Aliya feel like anything less than family. They had grown up together and Lena loved her friends fiercely, regardless of how much money they had.

"Ta-da!" Hana pointed to the box on her bed, practically glowing with excitement.

"A new phone?" Lena asked, a bit confused. "Is *that* the surprise?"

Aliya reached down and picked up the box. "Didn't you just get the last one replaced, like six months ago?" she asked, in an incredulous tone.

Hana, too preoccupied to notice that Aliya's tone was dripping with disdain, replied enthusiastically, "Yeah, but this is the newest one! And it comes in a different colour!" She proceeded to rip through the packaging while the other girls looked on quietly. They were happy for Hana, no doubt, but as Lena put her own phone away, broken screen and all, she couldn't help feeling a twinge of envy.

Aliya, in her typical nonchalant fashion, flicked her purple-tipped hair back and said, "Well, let's see what it can do then."

The next hour flew by, with the girls helping Hana connect the phone to her Apple ID, and downloading various apps, games and music. They marveled over the smallest features and tested out the camera with different filters. "These look amazing!" Hana was ecstatic, completely at odds with her usually calm and collected demeanor. Even Lena was impressed. The quality of pictures from her phone paled in comparison.

After some time, Aliya, tapping away at her phone, became visibly annoyed. "I can't connect the AirPods to my phone."

"Maybe you need to charge the AirPods," Hana suggested.

"It's not the AirPods," Aliya said. "It's the phone. It's super old."

"I would have sold you mine, but I think my parents are saving it for Sara for her next birthday."

"It's fine," Aliya said. "I'll figure something out. Anyway, I must leave soon. We have PE tomorrow. Do you have an extra bag I can borrow? I left mine at school."

Hana rummaged through her bulging walk-in closet and threw her a pink bag.

Aliya grimaced. "Seriously? You must have a hundred different bags. This one is pink. You know I don't wear pink."

"Whatever! The clothes aren't pink. It's just the bag," Lena said, as she threw a pillow in Aliya's face. "You know, there *are* other colours besides black."

Aliya smirked and threw the pillow back.

As they were getting ready to leave, Hana insisted on taking one more selfie with her best friends. They turned to face the window when Hana noticed a shadow in the hallway.

"Sara? Is that you?"

Sara came in timidly.

A loud blare from outside the window was Aliya's signal to leave. "That's my dad's 'Get-in-the-car-now' signal," Aliya blurted, as she rushed out of the room. A few seconds later, Lena got a text from her mother saying,

> *Aliya's dad will drop you home.*

"Gotta go!" And with a quick hug to both sisters, Lena rushed out.

On the car ride home, Lena felt her phone vibrate. She looked down and saw a message from Aliya, who was sitting in the front.

> *Don't you think a new phone is a bit much??? I mean, she just had the other one replaced a few months ago.*

Lena looked up and could see Aliya glancing at her through the side mirror, eyebrows just ever so slightly raised. She paused. She didn't know what to text back. What can you say when one of your closest friends knows nothing about waiting for hand-me-down clothes or gadgets? Lena's parents both worked to make sure that their kids would have good food and a warm bed every day. They never spoke about their financial difficulties, even though Lena knew that the brunt of their income went towards paying off their home and the impending pressure of college fees.

Aliya, on the other hand, was much more vocal about her family's financial woes. She lived alone with her father, who gained notoriety a decade ago by publishing a series of short stories. He had since struggled to match that success, which is why Aliya's list of complaints went from "Why is my dad always home?" to "What's the point of being a famous author if you still end up poor"?

Lena texted,

> *We are where God wants us to be.*

Aliya fired back,

> *So He wants us to be poor?*

Lena, already regretting responding to the first text, took longer to write something more thoughtful.

> *Everyone gets tested in different ways. Maybe this is Hana's test and that's what God wants for her.*

Aliya took a few minutes before texting:

> *I wouldn't mind THAT test.*

Lena didn't respond. *Neither would I*, she thought.

CHAPTER 3

GOD'S TEST

"Can you please just look under the seat, Ali?" Hana asked, pleadingly.

"I would if your lacrosse stick wasn't jabbing into my back," he responded.

"Ali," Salma said in a warning tone. Her eyes were closed as she rubbed the temples of her forehead, the telltale sign of an impending migraine.

Lena reached her arm around and pulled out Hana's phone from under the seat. It had dropped behind the seat (again) when Hana had been trying to show the girls a video.

"It's too big for you! Maybe you should give it to someone else who needs a new phone!" Aliya joked. "I'm sure your parents can afford to get you a new one."

Hana was used to hearing similar retorts and brushed it off. "It just takes some getting used to. Let's go so I can wallop you in dodgeball!"

Aliya smirked. "You wish!" Despite not participating in an after-school sport like Hana or Lena, Aliya was in excellent shape and took the opportunity to flex her strength in every gym class the girls shared together.

Once out of the car, the girls laughed and chatted as they made their way toward the changing rooms to get ready for PE. Lena fumbled with the zipper of her navy Reebok bag while Aliya muttered sourly about the pink bag Hana had lent her. She had apologized to Hana profusely about not returning the bag yet, but Hana didn't seem to mind. "Use it for as long as you need it. It goes great with black!", to which Aliya gave her a death stare. They threw their clothes and phones into their bags and headed to the gym.

Halfway there, Aliya suddenly turned and started jogging back towards the changing room.

"The gym is that way, genius," Lena said.

"Bathroom! Tell Coach Ahmed not to mark me absent!" Aliya answered, as she disappeared around the corner.

* * *

Forty-five minutes later, the girls emerged from a gruelling game of dodgeball, sore and sweaty. As they headed towards the showers, Lena caught a glimpse of some eighth-grade girls headed to the gym, including Sara, sporting a long-sleeve shirt under her PE uniform.

"You're going to boil in that!" Aliya called out to Sara as the girls piled into the changing room.

After showering and changing, Lena and Aliya fired review questions back and forth in preparation for their upcoming maths test. They passed by the locker room and were surprised to see Hana still standing by her locker. She hadn't showered or changed. Instead, she was rummaging through her bag, removing things and then putting them back quickly.

"No, no, no, no, no!" she was muttering to herself, with each "no" louder than the first. "This can't be happening!"

"What is it?" Lena asked.

Aliya stayed quiet and looked at her watch.

Hana looked up, distressed. "My phone," she said, her voice cracking as though she was about to cry. "It's gone."

CHAPTER 4

THE THREE MOVING DOTS

Weekends at the Khan household were often a busy time, what with the alarming amount of homework Lena was assigned and Ali's robotics competitions to prep for. Nevertheless, there was one stable constant amid the chaos: weekends were always a time for Qur'an study.

When the Qur'an teacher rang the doorbell, Ali would put every effort into making it look as though no one was home, by closing the curtains or stating, "No one is home!" This often earned him a sharp reprimand from his mother and a chuckle from the Qur'an teacher. Lena and Ali would then dutifully practice their verses with the tutor for an hour before completing their weekend chores and, finally, branching off to enjoy some free time.

Lena would be found curled up on the living room sofa, devouring her latest book, while Ali would spend hours talking to his friends online as they played *Fortnite*. Lena made it a point to leave her phone on silent during the weekends, so she could get the bulk of her reading done uninterrupted. With Hana's phone missing, however, Lena couldn't seem to concentrate on anything. She had never seen her friend so upset about anything. Lena and Aliya had helped Hana go through her locker and bag thoroughly, even risking the wrath of their math teacher when they arrived a few minutes late to class.

Where was her phone? Who would take it? Lena began scrolling aimlessly through her Instagram feed. *Maybe someone was using Hana's phone? Though how would they break through her complicated passcode?* She then saw a text from Aliya.

'Well? Did she find it?'

Careful to keep the phone in the middle of her book, Lena texted back:

'I don't know. She would have sent a message to the group chat if she did.'

Aliya:

'Tbh, I wouldn't be surprised if her parents replaced her phone before Monday.'

Lena:

'Me neither, but that's not the issue, is it? Who would take it?'

Lena sat back, waiting for a response. *Sure*, she thought, *Hana's family was well-off, and devices in their home were considered little more than toys, but Hana had become really attached to her new phone in the last few days*. It bothered Lena to see her friend so upset.

Lena looked down at her chat with Aliya. She could see that Aliya was typing something, but after a few minutes, the three moving dots disappeared and there was no reply.

Suddenly, she was startled by someone clearing their throat. Lena looked up and realized that her mother had been standing next to her for the last few minutes.

"Don't you have anything else to do?" her mother asked, her hand outstretched.

Lena handed her the phone, picked up her book and then walked away.

* * *

The afternoon passed by quickly, and by 4pm, Lena had finished all her homework and was ready to meet up with her friends. She approached her father, who was trying to help Ali with a complicated project for his robotics competition. Ali was clenching and unclenching his fists in frustration.

"Baba? Can you drop Aliya and me at Hana's house? She lost her phone and wants us to help her look for it."

Her father looked up. "Oh!? Sure, we can leave right after *Asr* prayer." Ali breathed an enormous sigh of relief.

Lena grabbed her favourite hijab. She called it her 'lucky' hijab because she was always wearing it whenever her team won a basketball match or she did well on a test.

When they pulled up in front of Aliya's house, Aliya climbed in, wearing a black hoodie with black Adidas track pants. Lena had opted to wear yoga leggings and a plaid shirt, just in case she needed to look in any nooks and crannies for the phone.

"Why the long face?" Aliya asked Lena when she saw her grim expression.

Lena shrugged, "I just hope Hana finds her phone, that's all."

"Me too," Aliya said, as she connected her phone to an outdated set of headphones. Lena looked at her friend with a quizzical expression. "It does the job," said Aliya quickly, before glancing away.

As they walked into Hana's room, the first thing they noticed was that the well-kept pristine appearance of it had been completely undone. The room looked as though it had been turned inside out. Hana, hair unkempt and still in her pajamas, even though it was late afternoon, was staring at the mess so intently that she didn't notice the girls enter. There were clear tracks worn into the carpet, as though she had been walking in circles around the room for some time.

Aliya and Lena were shocked by the sudden change in their best friend. It was as though someone had taken their calm friend, who was usually unperturbed by anything, and replaced her with a ghost of herself. Then, they heard a shuffling noise and saw Sara emerge from Hana's walk-in closet, clothes hanging off her shoulders as though she had been attacked by the fashion police.

"I looked everywhere. It's not in your room and not in your closet. Where else could it be?" Sara asked, looking at her older sister with concern.

Hana was sitting quietly on her bed, mumbling to herself, "I dropped it in the car. I checked the car. Then, I put it in my bag. I had it at school. I put it in my locker. I think I did."

There was an awkward silence. No one knew what to say.

Sara began brushing the rest of the clothes hanging off her. She reached down to untie a bunch of tangled scarves when Lena noticed a bruise on her wrist. "Sara, did you get hurt?"

Sara looked down and slowly exposed her wrist. "I tried something new yesterday in skating class and ended up crashing for my troubles. Never trying that one again!"

Hana was still being quiet, so the girls continued asking Sara about her ice skating, if only to make up for the silence.

"How long have you been skating?"

"How often do you practice?"

"Do you fall a lot?"

Sara answered all the questions, glancing towards Hana every so often with a pained expression. Hana just continued to stare at the mess of books, clothes, shoes and bags on the floor. She seemed completely and utterly lost. The girls tried hard not to check their own phones out of respect for Hana, but after exhausting the conversation about Sara's ice-skating lessons, they resorted to checking their social media.

Lena looked at Hana and waved to get her attention, a gesture which earned her a flash of annoyance. "Hey, snap out of it!" Lena commanded. "Take a break and try again later. When we get to school on Monday, let's go to lost property."

Hana's blank expression didn't change.

CHAPTER 5

BETWEEN THE LINES

On Sunday, Lena woke up to Ali jumping on her bed, shouting, "Today is the robotics competition! You promised you would come!"

How did his tone go from joyful to accusatory in the same breath? Lena wondered. She threw a pillow at him. "I know! I won't miss it, Insha'Allah. Just make sure you win."

Ali rolled his eyes. "You sound like Mama and Baba. Can you please keep Baba away from my project until the competition starts?"

Lena yawned, pawing at the bedside table in search of her phone. "Sure, when I get up." She brushed her hand over the end of the charger to unplug her phone, but it wasn't there. She sat up. "Where is my…?" She looked at Ali, who was dangling her phone by the attached PopSocket.

"Looking for this?" he said, a mischievous glint in his eye. Then he ran off, howling like a wolf.

"Ali! I'm going to kill you!" Lena yelled. She tried to run after him but tripped over her blanket, as well as a gigantic pile of stuffed animals that Ali had most definitely made while she was sleeping. "Give me back *my* phone!"

"Not until you get ready for the competition!" Ali was already downstairs, ensconced in the protection of his parents.

"Baba!" Lena yelled.

"Would you please calm down?" her father said in an exasperated tone. "Your phone isn't going anywhere."

Lena grumbled as she made her way to the bathroom and forcefully closed the door. *That's probably what Hana thought, too.*

* * *

When will this competition be over? wondered Lena. She was exhausted after Ali had woken her up so early. He had finally conceded and handed Lena back her phone, but not until she had kicked him under the table during breakfast, an act that had earned her a sharp scolding from her mother.

Should have brought a book, she thought, miserably, looking toward her parents, who were also not watching the competition. As she stared at her phone, trying to think of a way to connect to the Internet, it started to vibrate. She was startled to get a real call. *Who does that anymore?* she thought. *Oh, it's Hana's mom.*

"Assalaamu alaikum, Aunty Fatima.

"Wa Alaikum as Salaam, Lena. It's me, Hana! Just wait a second while I add Aliya to the call."

Lena glanced toward the group of final competitors. She proud of Ali and how he had made it to the finals. As annoying as he was, she was happy for him and was pleased that he possessed a unique talent – not that she would admit any of this, of course. Still, after-school activities were expensive and Lena's parents both worked to provide for the family. For herself, this provided the motivation to work hard at basketball practice, even putting in extra time before and after to ensure that she would get picked to play in every game. As a result, her parents took the time to come to her games and support her.

A few seconds later, Lena heard both Aliya and Hana's voice. "We searched the whole house. Papa even called the principal to get permission to search the school. We're here now but nothing has been turned in," she said, miserably.

"Wait a second," Aliya replied, "how did you get into school on a Sunday?"

"My dad knows the principal."

Aliya scoffed.

"But that's not the point!" Hana's voice was so close to a high-pitched wail that Lena had to hold the phone away from her ear. Hana started to hiccup. "It gets worse."

"What is it?" Lena asked, sympathetically.

"The ringer is completely off. Now there's no chance of finding it. And my parents are refusing to replace it. What do I do?" Hana began to cry.

Lena felt a nudge on her shoulder. Her father gestured for her to put her phone down because the awards ceremony was about to start. Lena held up one pleading finger, but her father shook his head. "I'm sorry, Hana. I really am, but I can't talk about this right now. We're at the robotics competition. I promise we'll discuss this at school tomorrow." Lena felt guilty but there was nothing more she could do.

"We'll figure it out," Aliya said, empathetically.

Lena's parents saw the troubled expression on her face and asked her what happened. They listened carefully, while paying close attention to the awards ceremony as well (clapping appropriately for Ali so that he heard them). Meanwhile, Lena filled them in as succinctly as she could.

When she had finished speaking, her mother gently said, "It doesn't seem as though the phone got lost at home. Someone must have taken the phone from her bag while you were all in the gym class. Do you remember if anyone was missing from the class?"

Lena thought back to that day. "No, we were evenly divided the whole time, except at the beginning when Aliya went back to the changing room to use the bathroom." As she said these words, she wished she could take them back.

She watched her brother go on stage to accept his prize (he even clapped for himself), but all the while, every disgruntled text about Hana's family, every flash of annoyance she had shown about her own phone and every snarky comment she had made about Hana came flooding into Lena's mind. *Was it Aliya? Did Aliya take the phone?*

CHAPTER 6

NAVIGATING THE FRIENDSHIP FIELD

She wouldn't do that. She just wouldn't do that. Lena kept repeating this over and over to herself. Her mind was reeling at the possibility that one of her best friends had taken her other best friend's new phone. *It's just a coincidence that the phone went missing after Aliya went to the bathroom during gym class. It couldn't be her, right?*

On the way home, Ali had the rare honour of sitting in the front seat next to Baba. They kept singing *We Are the Champions* at a volume that steadily rose with each chorus, until they were singing at the top of their lungs. Lena sat next to her mother in the back seat, who had her eyes closed. She was either sleeping or pretending to sleep. As Lena went over the events of the past few days, her mind kept going back to the same point. Aliya had been unhappy with her own phone for some time. She had made it painfully obvious on many occasions that she resented Hana's privileged life. She was jealous. There was only one way to get to the bottom of this.

"Baba, can you drop me at Aliya's house? I just want to go over some maths problems with her." *It's not a complete lie*, Lena thought. *We do need to go over a problem, but it's not exactly math-related.* She had to endure listening to a whole extra chorus of *We Are the Champions* before Lena's father even heard her request and made a left towards Aliya's neighbourhood.

When they reached Aliya's house, Lena hesitated before knocking on the door. *What do I say? 'Hey, did you get anything new lately? Maybe something that doesn't belong to you?'*

Just as Lena lifted her hand to knock, the door suddenly opened.

"Lena!" Aliya said, startled. "What are you doing here?" The words came out in a rush. She quickly stuffed something in a bag, one that Lena had never seen before. Aliya was dressed in her usual black attire, but today she didn't look so casual. She was wearing a black silky top under her suede jacket. Under her sleek black jeans, Lena noticed that she was sporting a new pair of black boots. *Where is she going?* Lena thought, suspiciously.

Lena looked back but saw that her family had already driven off. "Sorry! Are you going somewhere? My parents dropped me off on the way back from the competition." Lena quickly began to text her dad to swing back around to pick her up.

"Don't worry. We have a few minutes before my Uber arrives. I'll wait until you leave." Aliya said, checking the app. She closed the front door to wait with Lena on the porch. Aliya never had any reason to feel nervous around Lena, but today she was acting skittish. She fumbled with the keys and even dropped them, before finally locking the door.

"Stupid door," Aliya grunted, as she finally pried her key out of the lock. "Okay then, what's up?" she said, looking expectantly at Lena for an explanation as to why she had just shown up.

"Oh, um. I just wanted to stop by…" Lena was not expecting to be this tongue-tied with one of her best friends. They had known each other since third grade! Lena had once been intimidated by Aliya's tough exterior, with her black hair dyed purple at the tips, multiple piercings and goth aesthetic. She was sarcastic, bold and quick-witted, whereas Lena was cautious and more reserved. Still, underneath that hard shell was a softness, a layer of vulnerability that few people were privy to.

Aliya had a rebellious streak to the extent that when the women from the local *masjid* said one thing, Aliya tended to run in the opposite direction. She challenged the various teachers in their halaqa circle, demanding answers to questions that they simply didn't know how to respond to, garnering her reputation as a "bad influence" on the other Muslim girls.

Aliya's unyielding spirit coupled with a long-established rumour that her mother had left the family for questionable reasons made her and her father the local pariahs. No one knew much about Aliya's mother, when she had left or under what circumstances. Lena had never asked nor had Aliya ever freely divulged this information. Lena didn't feel like she needed to know either. After all, Aliya had earned her place as Lena's best friend time and time again.

When Dina, one of the fifth-grade bullies, 'accidentally' dropped some juice on top of Lena's books, Aliya had taken the juice box and promptly poured the rest of it over Dina's head. Out of pure humiliation, Dina didn't report the incident to anyone, but she made it a point to threaten every other girl in their class to stay clear of Aliya and Lena, too. Her plan certainly worked. Throughout sixth grade and the better part of seventh grade, the girls rarely got invited to parties. That is, until Hana moved to their school.

Joining the school in the middle of the year was unheard of. When students learned that the daughter of a pilot was joining seventh grade mid-year, it caused a stir. She had been drafted onto the HS lacrosse team (Lena and Aliya didn't know the school had one) before she even arrived. Everything about Hana, her clothing, her loosely draped designer scarves, her bags, her devices and, not to mention, her family's ornate mansion in one of the nicest areas in town, reeked of privilege. The only thing that did not exude any semblance of elitism was her attitude.

Hana had spent much of her life around people whose lives resembled a perfectly filtered Instagram shot. On her first day of school, Hana practically floated through the cafeteria like a gazelle, her designer bag slung carelessly over her shoulder and expensive sunglasses perched delicately on her loose scarf. She plopped herself down next to Aliya and Lena unceremoniously, who, by the look on their faces, might have mistaken her for an alien that had accidentally landed at their table.

"I heard they have some really great chocolate chip cookies in the cafeteria. Maybe one of you can get one for me?" Hana asked, coolly, as she stared at Lena.

Lena blushed when she realized that she had been staring at Hana for the last few seconds. She wasn't the only one. The whole cafeteria was now looking in their direction, some from a side angle and some were just outright gawking. Dina was glaring in a way that looked like she might combust at any minute.

Lena paused before answering, knowing full well she wasn't going to get pushed into doing anything for anyone, no matter how much influence they had. At the same time, she didn't want to insult the new girl on her first day of school. Aliya, on the other hand, had no reservations.

"They are really good," Aliya said, with a smirk. "Too bad you don't have one."

Before anyone realized what was happening, Hana had snatched up Aliya's cookie and taken a bite from it. Everyone around their table gasped and looked on with greedy eyes, waiting to see the impending havoc that was sure to ensue.

Aliya stood up, eyes flashing as though she was about to punch the new girl, when, suddenly, Hana choked. Her eyes began to bulge and her face started turning red. She only uttered one word – "peanut" – before she ran out of the cafeteria. Some students were aghast and followed Hana's departing figure with amazement, while others went back to eating their lunches as though nothing had even happened.

Lena, whose brother also had a food allergy, did not hesitate. She quickly grabbed her things and the items Hana had left behind and got up. Aliya was in a state of shock, but she wasn't one to argue with Lena as she snapped furiously, "Are you coming or what?"

Together, they ran towards a frantic Hana, who was roaming the halls because she had no idea where the medical office was. Lena grabbed her by the scarf and steered her in the right direction and toward the nurse, who had already been alerted by the cafeteria staff. Luckily, Hana had detected the peanut as soon as it had touched her mouth so most of it had been spat out already. Hana's mother, Fatima, came to pick her up before taking her to the doctor, meanwhile threatening a lawsuit for selling cookies with traces of peanuts. As she was leaving, Lena and Aliya noticed another girl who strongly resembled Fatima. They later found out that the girl was Sara, Hana's younger sister.

The next day, Hana did not come to school, so Lena took the initiative to visit her at home. Aliya sighed dramatically but agreed to go. When they entered Hana's house, they immediately noticed a huge crystal chandelier hanging high above the grand foyer. The living room was elaborately decorated with beautiful works of art, which they later discovered were painted by Fatima herself.

The rest of the house, to Lena and Aliya's surprise, looked like theirs. Sports equipment was scattered throughout the house. Fatima kept her art supplies out in case she felt "inspired in the moment", Hana had explained, rolling her eyes. Sara enjoyed baking in the kitchen so it was not unusual to find the countertop covered with a thin layer of flour. Hana's dad, being a pilot, was usually away due to work, but his presence was felt by the massive DVD collection of action movies he had collected over the years, showcased prominently in the family room.

Hana was pleasantly surprised by the girls' visit and promptly asked them to stay and watch a movie. Lena remembered thinking that perhaps Hana only wanted to become friends with her and Aliya because the girls were from middle-class backgrounds, thus making Hana stand apart even more. Over time, though,

Lena came to realize that Hana was the most honest, frank and down-to-earth person that she had ever met. Hana loved her lifestyle, no doubt. There were times when she was oblivious to her friends' economic circumstances, like when she would purchase the most expensive item at a restaurant, or would buy clothes on top of clothes at the mall, unperturbed by Lena and Aliya's discomfort. At the same time, she would tell the girls to buy things for themselves, even convincing Aliya that grey was a type of black. Also, for someone who got squeamish over small injuries, Hana had stood stalwart during hospital visits when Lena had her appendix removed. She was insightful enough to see right through any lens, and view a person for who they were, not what they were worth.

Hana had proven herself as a fierce friend, committed to Lena and Aliya as they navigated the minefield of middle-school friendships. Thankfully, when the girls had transitioned into high school, their friendship had become stronger. *Which is exactly why*, Lena thought, as her family drove home, *the thought of suspecting Aliya of stealing Hana's phone is so difficult to swallow.*

CHAPTER 7

A BETRAYAL ON TWO FRONTS

"It's like Coach Ahmed purposely chooses dodgeball on the days I'm not wearing my contacts," Lena grumbled, pushing her glasses up her nose, slick with sweat as she pulled her school clothes out of her bag. It was two days later and the girls had just finished a PE class.

"I think I forgot to use deodorant," Hana said, lifting her arms and taking a sniff.

"Ew!" both girls exclaimed.

"What difference does that make?" Aliya said, playfully. "You're both ugly either way."

Lena scrunched her sweaty gym towel into a ball and pretended to pass it like a basketball to Aliya. Because she wasn't wearing her contacts, however, she missed getting anywhere near her target. Instead, the towel hit the pink bag that Hana had let Aliya borrow, causing it to fall to the floor with a thud. Something fell out of the bag and slid right in front of Hana.

"Good job, Aliya. You probably broke your... phone." But Hana was not holding Aliya's phone. She was looking at her own, the phone that she had lost a week before. The screen was slightly damaged from the fall, but otherwise it was in perfect condition.

Both Lena and Hana looked at Aliya and saw that Aliya's face had turned ashen, as though all the colour had been drained out of it.

"What is this?" Hana asked, impassively, though it was clear that she was struggling to keep her emotions in check.

"That's not my phone," Aliya quickly replied.

"Yeah, I know it's not your phone. It's mine. What's it doing in your bag?" Hana asked.

"That's not my bag," Aliya relayed.

"Yes, Aliya. It's my bag – the bag I let you borrow," Hana retorted.

"Yes, I… know." Aliya was stumbling for words. "I know you let me borrow it… but I didn't put the phone in there."

The usual raucous laughter that punctuated the changing room had died down. Girls were now peeking behind their lockers to see the events unfolding between Aliya and Hana.

"Well, then," Hana said, snatching her scarf from the bench, "tell me this. How did *my* phone end up in *my* gym bag, which *you* conveniently borrowed?"

"I don't know!" Tears had started to well up in Aliya's eyes. "I mean, I saw it in the bag right before gym…" she stopped, suddenly realizing that she had incriminated herself.

"Wait, so you knew where the phone was an hour ago? But you didn't know where the phone was before that?" Hana was now close to shouting.

Lena jumped in, hoping to allay the situation before it escalated into an ugly fight. Judging by the anger on Hana's face and Aliya's guilty expression, she was too late.

"Don't look at me. Don't talk to me. Ever." Hana stormed off and a few seconds later, they heard the door to the changing room slam.

Lena grabbed an unresisting Aliya. She'd noticed that some of the other girls had pulled out their phones during the fight and started taking videos, so she snapped, "Don't you dare! Unless Coach Ahmed wants to know who was making a video in the changing room." The girls slowly put their phones away and Lena dragged her friend halfway across the school.

"Where are we going?" Aliya mumbled, but Lena remained silent.

As they marched through the school, Aliya vaguely recognized the baseball field on the other side of campus, close to where the middle-schoolers ate lunch every day. Out of the corner of her eye, she saw a bewildered Sara give a tentative wave in their direction, but Lena could not be distracted. She was determined to get to the bottom of this.

They walked past the field and back into the school using a door that Aliya recognized as the middle-school locker room. The locker room was connected to the bathroom. After checking underneath each stall to make sure that no one was hiding inside, Lena confronted Aliya.

"What happened?" Lena practically hissed at Aliya. "How did the phone end up in your bag?"

Aliya flinched. She hadn't expected an interrogation from Lena. "When I got my clothes out, I felt something in the bag. I knew it wasn't my phone because I'd left my phone in my backpack before we left for PE. I didn't want to take a chance after Hana's phone had been taken," she said, defensively.

Lena raised an eyebrow, which Aliya interpreted as her cue to continue.

She sighed. "I don't know how it ended up there. I just borrowed the pink bag because I was used to it and it wasn't like Hana needed it anyway. The phone wasn't in the bag when I borrowed it, I swear!"

"If you saw the phone in the bag before PE, why didn't you say anything then?" Lena asked.

"Because I was shocked! I didn't know how it ended up there! I didn't know how to explain it to Hana. Like, 'Hey, Hana. Guess what I just found in my gym bag?' So, I just stuffed it back in the bag and figured I would deal with it later." She sat down and started rocking back and forth, a telltale indication that her anxiety was kicking in.

Lena closed her eyes. *Think.*

"Aliya," she said, trying to muster some sympathy in her voice, "I know that you were unhappy with your phone. You've been complaining about it for ages. Do you think, maybe, you want to tell the truth on this one? You know I'm here for you."

Aliya stopped rocking. She stood up and looked her best friend straight in the eye. "You know, I'm used to people accusing me of things. I've heard the *masjid* women talk about how I was such a bad kid that even my mother walked out on me. Or that she left because my dad lost all the money he made from publishing his book and couldn't think of what to write anymore. But stealing? From my best friend? I never thought I would hear that from you."

The words stung Lena but she refused to show any remorse. If Hana's phone had been taken and Aliya had stolen it, then Hana deserved justice. She deserved an apology.

Even after Aliya left, Lena stayed in the changing room until she heard the students coming back inside. She wiped her tears and walked out, her heart heavy with the knowledge that her two best friends were hurting and there was nothing she could do about it.

CHAPTER 8

A CLOSER LOOK

The weekend came faster than Lena expected. On Saturday, during breakfast, Ali announced that he had invited three friends over for a movie night, prompting Lena to request a sleepover at Hana's house. Now that Aliya was no longer on speaking terms with either of them, Lena was spending more and more time with Hana. There were moments when the girls keenly felt Aliya's absence. At those times, Hana would rush to call Sara and have her hang out with them before Lena could bring up the topic.

"You can't avoid this forever," Lena protested when Sara left them alone to brush her teeth. "We need to talk about this."

"No, you need to talk about it. I don't want to hear about it," Hana said, scrolling through her Snapchat.

"Hana, when has Aliya ever lied about anything? She's been your best friend for two years and she's never done anything to hurt you. Maybe this is all just a big misunderstanding."

"Maybe before, but not recently," Hana muttered.

"What's that supposed to mean?" Lena demanded.

"Are you saying that Aliya has been completely honest? About everything?"

"Well…"

"Here, look at this snap. A friend of mine sent it to me last weekend and I took a screenshot."

Lena peered down and saw a picture of two girls from Hana's old public school standing in front of Maison, a fancy restaurant in the city district.

"What does this have to do with anything?"

"Look closer."

Lena took the phone and enlarged the picture. She then looked at the date. It was taken on the Sunday evening of the robotics competition, the day when Lena had stopped by Aliya's house to confront her. Lena hadn't questioned Aliya on where she was going with her new clothes and bag, or what she had hidden in her bag. She didn't have to. The answer was right in front of her on the screenshot. Aliya was sitting in a restaurant with an older man, head tilted and smiling like Lena had never seen her smile before.

"I didn't know how to ask her," Hana said, quietly. "I was going to. You must believe me. I wasn't going to think the worst about my best friend without me asking her why she was having dinner with an older guy. And then, two days later, when my phone shows up in her bag, I just... lost it." Hana sighed and fell back on her bed.

Lena knew Aliya like the back of her hand. Aliya would never keep secrets from her, especially not something like this. *Who was this man she was meeting? And why?*

"You're right, though," Hana said, as she climbed into her huge four-poster bed and used her phone to dim the lights. "I do need to talk to her."

"No, we need to talk to her," Lena said, bitterly, as she took off her glasses and lay back on the extra mattress next to Hana's bed. "She's been keeping things from both of us."

The girls lay quietly in bed, mulling over the puzzle of who Aliya had been dining with and how Hana's phone had come into her possession. It was late when the girls drifted off to sleep, their thoughts plagued with the notion that maybe they didn't know their best friend as well as they thought they did.

CHAPTER 9

AN EMPTY SEAT

"Quick, the show is about to start. Someone pass me a samosa."

"Where is my lemonade?"

"Mama, I have to go to the bathroom."

"Well, hold it in. No one's taking you."

"I can go by myself!"

"Ask your father. And get me a Diet Coke on the way back. No wait, make that a Perrier."

Hana and Lena's families were at the local ice rink, seated in the middle row for the Frozen-themed ice-skating show. From their angle, they would have a perfect view of all the performers as they displayed their skills in figure skating, Sara included. Hana and Sara's father, Khalid, had secured tickets for the show weeks in advance. He had personally invited Lena and Aliya's families to join in. At the time, Aliya had said that her father would be busy at a writer's convention, but that she would attend.

Lena looked wistfully at the empty seat between her and Hana. She half-hoped that Aliya would show up, just to fill the gaping void she had felt in her heart since they had started avoiding each other at school.

Suddenly, the lights dimmed and Lena turned her attention towards the rink.

Each of the skaters did their own version of various songs from *Frozen*, during which Ali kept grumbling, "Ew!" When Sara came on the ice, she was dressed modestly. She had opted to forego the tight Lycra outfit customary of figure skaters and instead wore dark blue leggings with an aqua long-sleeved tunic that was adorned in sequins. Her makeup was done simply, with just a hint of blue eyeshadow.

Being petite, Sara looked so small on the ice that hardly anyone was looking in her direction. There was more chattering than usual at the start of Sara's performance, but that didn't seem to bother Sara. She was looking at her family.

Everyone waved enthusiastically and Hana let out a loud whistle. Sara blushed and got into position for her performance of *Show Yourself*, a song she had chosen from the *Frozen 2* soundtrack. As the instrumental started, Sara started moving in small circles, transitioning into larger and larger sweeps of the ice until each turn was followed by a dizzying spin that Lena couldn't follow. Every hand gesture was precise, every twist and turn was unexpected, and within a minute into the song, her performance had captivated the entire audience. Everyone watched in stunned silence as the music reached a crescendo, during which Sara's small leaps on the ice turned into jumps. She moved as though she was made for the ice.

Lena suddenly felt a splash on her leg.

"Ali, you kicked my lemonade." Hana hissed, clearly annoyed.

"Well, maybe you should have been holding it in your hand," Ali retorted.

"Quiet! Sara is still performing!" Fatima scolded, not noticing that she was videotaping the whole conversation.

"Ugh, my shoes are soaking. I'm going to go wash them off before they get completely ruined," Hana whispered, before quietly moving past Lena's seat and heading toward the bathroom.

Lena wiped off her clothes as best as she could and turned her attention back to the rink, where Sara was finishing her performance. When the music finally stopped, Sara received a standing ovation. She clasped her hands together as a show of thanks and looked towards her friends and family. Both Lena and Hana's families were cheering the loudest.

As everyone began to sit down for the next performance, Sara remained where she was, scanning the seats, evidently looking for Hana. Lena mouthed "Bathroom" and Sara nodded. As she glided back to where the other skaters were seated, Lena noticed that her shoulders were drooped ever so slightly from exhaustion.

* * *

That night, Fatima hosted a party to celebrate Sara's performance. She came close to inviting every eighth-grade girl until Sara saw the guest list and vehemently said, "No!" Her mother finally relented and Sara only invited a few girls, including some of the other girls from her figure skating class. Even then, it took some cajoling on Hana and Lena's part to convince Sara to come downstairs and join the party. Hana attempted to grab her arm to drag her downstairs, but Sara jumped back.

"It's fine," she said, laughing, "I'm coming! Tell Mama and Papa that I'll be down in a minute."

Lena and Hana made their way downstairs and chatted about which appetizers they would try first. Fatima had spared no expense on the food and decorations. Since the theme of the skating show had been *Frozen*, Fatima had taken it upon herself to deck the house with a dazzling array of whites and blues. There were glittery streamers over every window. Thankfully, Hana had stopped her mother from ordering the Elsa, Anna, and Olaf cut-outs. "They're for the photobooth and selfies!" her mother relayed. "No! They're for a five-year-old birthday party, Mama!" Hana had insisted.

Lena and Hana became so preoccupied with munching on the various assortments of appetizers that they didn't notice Aliya until they heard her voice behind them say, "Hey."

Aliya had ditched her black-on-black ensemble for a long grey dress with three-quarter-length sleeves. She wore black boots, the same ones that Lena had seen on the day of the robotics tournament. Her beautiful black hair was pulled back into a ponytail and her purple tips had been re-dyed, now matching the deep purple earrings hanging from her ears. Evidently, Aliya had put a lot of effort into looking nice for this party.

Lena smiled at her and then turned her head to Hana, who was taken aback by Aliya's sudden appearance.

"I didn't know you were coming," Hana stammered.

"Neither did I. Until your mother personally called my dad and insisted that if we didn't show up for the performance, we should at least come for the afterparty."

Hana glowered at her mother, who was making a point *not* to look in the girls' direction.

"In any case," Aliya continued, "I wanted to come and meet you both. I have something to say." She looked at Hana first. "I'm sorry that I stole your phone. I was jealous that you always got such nice gifts from your parents and I wanted to know what it felt like to have one of my own. I shouldn't have taken it and I'm sorry." Aliya spoke the words quickly, as though she wanted to get them out before she regretted it.

She turned to Lena. "You were right to suspect me of taking the phone. I should have confessed when the time was right and I'm sorry." She apologized to Hana one more time and asked for her forgiveness.

"Of course I forgive you! I missed you!" Hana threw her arms around her. Then, Aliya went to hug Lena.

"Wait," Lena stopped her. Aliya took a step back, eyeing her friend warily. "You're coming to apologize now? It's been three weeks and you haven't said a word. Why now?"

Lena could sense that something wasn't right. Aliya wasn't one to go on and on with apologies. For all the years that Lena had known her, Aliya had hated admitting she was wrong, but when she did, she admitted it right away.

Aliya's eyes widened. "I…" Her answer was interrupted by a sudden burst of applause from the living room. Sara had finally emerged from her room.

Salma was reciting a long and exhaustive list of *duas* for Sara while everyone in the room politely said "Amen" to each as they tried to eat. Sara looked positively radiant in her pink floral dress. She made her way to Hana, who was trying to post pictures of the party decorations on her Instagram story. However, her wi-fi wasn't working, so she moved away to find a better connection. Lena leaned forward and gave Sara a hug, squeezing her affectionately. Sara winced and Lena quickly moved back.

"Sorry! I just realized you must be sore from your performance, which was amazing!"

Aliya patted Sara stiffly on the back.

"Congratulations on your performance."

At that moment, Hana came back to the group.

"Done! How's it going, little sis? Enjoying the attention?" she smirked.

Sara, shook her head, glancing at Aliya and then to her mother, who was frantically trying to get her to greet everyone in the room. "Catch you later," Sara said, smiling, though her smile did not reach her eyes.

As she walked away, an uneasy silence fell over the girls. Aliya started shifting her weight from side to side and muttered, "I'm going to find my dad."

"No, you're not," Lena said, assertively. Aliya and Hana looked blankly at her. She indicated to the girls to follow her upstairs.

When the girls entered Hana's room, Lena turned to Aliya and said, "Spill it."

"Spill what?" Aliya said, averting Lena's keen stare. "I already apologized. What do you want from me?"

"I know you didn't take the phone."

"You do?" Aliya was astonished.

"You do?" Hana repeated.

"I know that you were annoyed about your own phone and that Hana had a brand-new one that she didn't need, but I know you would never take it. Just tell us what really happened."

"It was me!"

Aliya had never been good at lying. Hana's eyes narrowed, and she stood up and looked right at her. Aliya moved back, if only to avoid stepping on Hana's massive stuffed animal collection at her feet.

"Did you steal my phone?" Hana asked, quietly.

Aliya looked at her and said decidedly, "No."

Hana nodded. "Then, who took it?"

"I can't tell you," Aliya mumbled.

"You can't or won't?" Lena asked.

Aliya looked at both of them. "I won't. I promised I would not tell."

Lena and Hana were stunned. "Promised who?"

"She made a promise to *me*," came a voice from the doorway. All three girls whirled around and watched as Sara entered the room.

CHAPTER 10

SHOW YOURSELF

"You took my phone?" Hana said, trying to keep her voice even. "What? Why?"

Sara looked helplessly at Aliya, who stepped in between the girls as though to defend Sara. Hana was bewildered by this notion. Lena's mind was still trying to process the confession. Sara, Hana's innocent younger sister, had stolen her own sister's phone and then tried to frame Hana's best friend for it?

Sara put a hand on Aliya's arm and said, gently, "It's okay, I have to tell her. I… I have to tell someone," she said, as her voice wavered.

Aliya looked at her straight in the eyes and said, "I'm here for you, whatever you need." She then sat down next to Lena on the bed. Lena was baffled, looking back at both Aliya and Sara, trying to figure out when they had become such good friends.

It was then that Hana exploded. "Would someone please explain to me what is going on?!"

"It was me!" Sara said. "I took your phone when you went for PE."

"I figured that much out, but why?"

"I just…" Sara looked miserable. "I just wanted you to pay attention to me. You already had your best friends and then when you got your new phone, you just…" She couldn't bring herself to say the words.

"Ignored you?" Lena asked, gently.

Sara nodded, tears streaming down her face. "I couldn't stand it. I don't know why I couldn't. I just wanted you to look at me – not your friends, not your phone – me. But you wouldn't. When I saw how sad you were about the phone, I felt bad. I knew I had to get it back to you, somehow. So, I…" she stopped, looking sheepish.

"She put the phone in my bag, the same way she had taken it out, while we were in PE," Aliya continued. Sara looked down. "I knew it wasn't me, obviously, but I didn't figure it out until later that day." She glanced at Lena.

"When you confronted me in the bathroom, I walked out through the changing rooms and I saw Sara. I saw her…" That's when Aliya stopped. She stared intently at Sara to finish the story.

"Her what? You guys are terrible at this! Enough with the suspense," Hana said, irritated.

"My scars."

Slowly, Sara peeled off the cardigan that covered the arms under her short-sleeved dress. Hana gasped and Lena jumped back. Sara's arms were riddled with cuts and bruises, some of them fresh and some that had faded. Hana looked at her sister, then took a step back and fell onto her bed. This was Sara, the quiet, talented sister, who was a constant force in Hana's life. Now, looking at her arms, which Sara was obviously not used to exposing, she felt like she didn't know her sister at all.

How long has Sara been hiding this? thought Lena.

Hana couldn't bring herself to say anything. She just continued to stare at her sister.

"I saw the marks in the changing room. They looked…" Aliya's voice suddenly cracked. "They looked like the marks that my mother used to have on her arms and on her back. She would pinch and cut herself, like she had this pain inside her and she was trying to cut that pain out. None of us knew how to help. I don't think my mother even understood why she did it. My dad was so busy with his tours and book signings. I was too young to understand what was happening to her. Her friends, the "aunties" from the *masjid*," Aliya said bitterly, "thought that my dad was the one hurting her. She didn't want anyone thinking such terrible things about him. He loved her, but he didn't know what to do. So, she left to get help.

At least, that's what she said she was doing. Her last words to me and Baba were, 'This is my problem and I must fix it, not you'. We haven't heard from her since I was ten."

Sara covered her arms and sat down in the corner of the room, hugging her knees, as though she was trying to make herself smaller. Lena looked at Hana, indicating that she should go to her sister. However, Hana bore the same expression as when she'd lost her phone – only this time, she looked as though she'd lost her sister.

Aliya sat down next to Hana and clasped her hands. "I know that you're feeling hurt and betrayed, but this isn't about you. This issue is bigger than you, me, Lena and everything you know. This is about helping Sara overcome this illness. Don't treat her as though this is her problem. Don't do to Sara what my mother did to herself," Aliya pleaded, as silent tears streamed down her cheeks. "She isolated herself, which drove her away from everyone who cared about her. You need to put your hurt aside and focus on Sara."

Hana stood up and walked across the room to where Sara was huddled on the floor. She touched her ever so gently, without malice or revulsion. Sara flinched, anticipating a severe reprimand for how much damage she had caused. Instead, Hana said, faintly, "I love you, Sara. I love you with all my heart. I wish… I wish you had spoken to me about how you were feeling. I never meant to ignore you. I just sometimes get carried away with… basically everything. I want to help in whatever way I can. Just please talk to me."

She sat on the floor next to Sara. For once, all cell phones had been forgotten on the bedside table. Lena and Aliya quietly shuffled out of the room and went downstairs to join the rest of the party.

"Where's Sara?" Ali asked at the bottom of the stairs. He had somehow removed half the balloons in the house and created a long, billowing superhero cape that the adults kept tripping over and bursting.

"She's tired and taking a break in Hana's room," said Lena.

"But I want to show Sara my cape!" Ali whined. Lena rubbed her eyes, which were dry from her contacts. She wished she had worn her glasses.

"I just said she's tired and probably doesn't want to see your ridiculous cape," Lena snapped at her little brother.

Ali glared at his sister, until Aliya chimed in, "Why do you want to only show it to Sara? Do you like her?" she smirked. Ali's face turned red.

"No way! She smells, like all girls!" he said before running away, his balloon-cape bobbing after him.

The girls looked at each other and chased after a squealing Ali, laughing hysterically as they popped the rest of the balloons on his cape.

CHAPTER 11

SECRETS UNLOCKED

In the days that followed, Lena and Aliya spent time catching up on everything, from school assignments they had missed doing together, to social media accounts they followed, to speculating who would be Dina's next victim. Hana still spent time with her friends, but sometimes she'd have lunch with Sara or attend school plays with her. Sometimes they'd sit on the bleachers after school, just talking. Before, Sara would walk with her shoulders slumped forward and eyes cast down on the pavement, but now she had a bounce in her step. She was always smiling and looking happily at her sister – whose phone remained firmly at the bottom of her bag.

Hana's parents were finally made aware of Sara's struggle with depression. Sara and Hana sat down with them and Sara opened up about everything that had happened that month. Fatima broke down in tears, promising that they would seek help for Sara together, and Khalid promised to spend less hours at work and more time at home with his daughters.

A week later, all four girls were hanging out at Lena's house. Ali, after having been embarrassed by Aliya at the party, turned red when he saw Sara and made it a point to not speak to her at all.

"What did I do?" Sara asked, quizzically, to which Ali responded by slamming his door shut.

Hana was cleaning out pictures from her phone when she came across the screenshot of Aliya at the restaurant.

"Aliya, since we're being honest with each other, can you explain this?"

Aliya peered at the picture, not looking embarrassed at all. Lena held her breath and waited expectantly.

"That was taken at the Maison restaurant! I remember that night."

The girls glanced at each other and then at Aliya.

Sara looked up. "What were you doing there?"

Aliya put her phone away. "I'm not going to tell you. I'm going to show you!"

She marched down the stairs, leaving the girls no other choice but to grab their scarves and bags and follow her. They walked a few blocks over to Aliya's house, pestering her the whole time.

"It's a surprise!" Aliya said, laughingly, refusing to give the girls any hint of what they were about to see.

When they reached Aliya's house, she ordered them to close their eyes before entering. "Okay? Now, ready… open your eyes!"

The girls opened their eyes and gasped. Inside the living room were stacks upon stacks of books, freshly printed and ready to ship. Lena picked up one of the books and saw that the author was none other than Aliya's father.

"He got a book published! Why didn't you say anything?" Lena said, as she turned the book over in her hands.

Aliya flipped her hair back. "I couldn't! Baba made me promise not to say anything until the checks had been cleared and the books had been shipped. He's been taking me to all of his events because he didn't want me to feel…" Aliya stopped and looked at Sara.

"Alone," Sara continued and Lena knew right away that both girls had a deep understanding of what that felt like.

"Well, that explains the new clothes and shoes," Hana said.

The clothing, thought Lena – "but that doesn't explain the guy in the restaurant."

"You mean the agent for the publishing company?" Aliya asked, incredulously. "You think I would have dinner with an older man, just like that? My dad would kill me!"

"But your dad wasn't there," Lena pointed out.

Aliya took the phone from Hana and pulled up the picture. When she zoomed in, the girls noticed the shoulder of someone sitting next to the older man, the person whom Aliya was actually smiling at – her dad.

Hana and Lena looked sheepishly at one another. Sara rolled her eyes at them.

* * *

Later that night, as Lena lay in bed, she thought about everything that had happened in the past month. The phone theft, the betrayal and the awareness that someone so close was silently suffering from a serious mental health illness. It made Lena realize that the journey into high school was not going to be easy. Already, the people close to her were facing tests that she had never considered in middle school.

As she drifted off to sleep, she prayed that God would give her, Aliya, Hana and Sara the ability to overcome these obstacles and strengthen their friendships.

A WOUND LIKE NO OTHER
(A NOVELLA)

CHAPTER 1

The stench was practically unbearable, wafting from the inside of the house down the brick-lined pathway in front of it. As ten-year-old Aliya drew nearer, her overnight bag on her shoulder, she glanced down at the flowerbed. The purple geraniums that her mother had so carefully planted a few days prior had wilted and the leaves had taken on a yellowish tint. The smell was now so bad that by the time she found her house key, tucked between her pajamas and pillow, Aliya felt like she was going to pass out. She opened the door and nearly gagged.

"Mama?" Aliya called out.

No answer.

She called again, louder. "Mama?"

Again, no response.

Aliya made her way through every room, clutching her bag like it was some sort of anchor. As she did so, her voice became louder and louder until she found herself screaming, as though the pitch of her voice could summon her mother from whatever depths of depression she had sunk into this time.

The note lay folded upright on the bed. She read it, her bag dropping to the floor, and cried.

CHAPTER 2

"I'm home!"

Aliya kicked open the front door. She threw her bag and cardigan unceremoniously into the living room and plopped down on the sofa, still in her white Converse sneakers.

Her mother called out, "In the kitchen… and put your things away *properly.*"

Aliya groaned and made her way to the kitchen, picking up her things along the way and placing her shoes by the door.

"*Salaam.* How was your day?" Her mother asked absent-mindedly, staring intently at her phone while stirring the pasta on the stove.

"*Wa Alaikum salaam*, Mama. My day? My day! Where do I start?" Aliya huffed, dramatically.

Her day had started off well, despite her late night of gaming. It had begun to go downhill when her Spanish teacher had quizzed the students on how to order food. "Wouldn't you just ask in English?" Aliya asked, which earned her a trip to the vice-principal's office *and* the guidance counselor.

On her way back from the office, where she'd received the usual talk about respecting teachers and being more responsible, Aliya had walked past a group of fifth-grade boys. They were supposed to be completing a group assignment but were instead discussing the latest *Fortnite* update. Aliya couldn't resist the opportunity to voice her opinions on the matter and so she joined the heated discussion. After a few minutes, however, the boys had fallen silent.

Yeah, that's right. Even girls can game, she'd thought, smugly, then she felt a tap on her shoulder. She turned and saw the guidance counselor standing behind her. Begrudgingly, Aliya made her way back to the principal's office.

"We've discussed this topic over and over," Aliya's mother said, scooping some pasta onto plates for them. They both sat down to eat. "I let you play as long as you want because *you* have to learn how to balance your schoolwork *and* your hobbies. I can't do that for you."

"I'll work harder," Aliya said, before choking on a mouthful of hot pasta, which her mother had seemingly forgotten to warn her about. They fell into an easy silence. This was the norm in Aliya's home. Aliya played hours of video games while her mother looked the other way, too preoccupied with her real estate business to regulate her.

When Aliya's parents would receive emails from her teachers, they would scold her and attempt to dole out some punishment such as "no socializing" (Aliya didn't have any friends anyway, nor a phone to keep in touch with anyone) or "no late night gaming" (which didn't interfere with afternoon gaming). Only Aliya's father disapproved of her hobby, but luckily he wasn't around much to scold her. Having recently published a book on writing, Jalal spent weeks on the road, marketing his book and giving lectures on creative writing at various colleges.

"She's not going to play these games forever. Besides, I thought you liked girls who were headstrong and confident," her mother had playfully said after Jalal's last reprimand, when he had shut off the wi-fi over a missing Social Studies report.

"She's starting middle school next year, Basma. Her work habits will set the tone for high school and eventually college," her father replied.

Aliya only half listened when her parents argued over her habits. The more they had to say about her hobbies, the less she wanted to hear about it.

CHAPTER 3

One evening, Aliya finished her chores and sat down to eat with her family. As they dug into a delicious meal of roasted salmon made by Aliya's father, her parents discussed some recent developments in her mother's real estate business.

"Reem and I are meeting with Khalda next week. Turns out she is looking to move, so we might be putting the house on the market any day now. You know that house is going to sell quick!" her mother said, excitedly.

"Khalda's house is huge! Can we live there?" Aliya asked, already picturing an entire room dedicated to gaming.

"It's great that you're doing this," her father said, carefully, "but we really don't need the money. I've made enough from the book sales to open a separate account for Aliya's college fund. Maybe it's time to scale back and spend more time with Aliya, since she clearly needs some discipline. She also needs to finish her green beans," he said, frowning at the intricate design she had constructed with her vegetables.

"It's a *Minecraft* emerald!" Aliya exclaimed. "And I can manage my own screen time!" She folded her arms *over each other* to show her displeasure at yet *another* conversation about her.

"Yes, of course, dear," said her mother, nonchalantly scratching her wrist.

Aliya gave her mother a half-smile, knowing full well that her mom would never stop her from gaming. Just then, she noticed that the skin her mom was scratching looked raw. "Mama, you're bleeding!"

Her father quickly got up and opened the medicine cabinet, soon finding disinfectant and a bandage. With a gentleness that Aliya rarely witnessed in her encounters with her father, he wrapped the wound and kissed it. Mama smiled and, in that moment, Aliya saw a glimpse of love and tenderness that made her feel warm and happy.

As she climbed into bed, with its Minecraft-themed comforter and assortment of stuffed animals, she thought about the events of the evening. Yes, her parents argued. Yes, they disagreed on things. At the end of the day, though, she had two parents that loved her and wanted what was best for her, in their own ways.

CHAPTER 4

The next day, half of the fifth-grade boys were discussing the next *Fortnite* tournament. Aliya had asked almost every one of them to add her to their squad, but they either looked at her as though she were an alien or just walked away, muttering "Girls don't play *Fortnite*."

She only had one chance left: Ahmed, her lab partner and the only boy who didn't treat her like she had three heads.

"You know I can't let you on my squad," Ahmed said, quietly, trying not to attract attention as they stood side by side, taking measurements of their bean plant. "All the boys will think you're my…" Ahmed stopped and his face turned beet red. Aliya rolled her eyes and said, "Fine, but don't expect my help!" before stalking away. Some boys behind snickered and Aliya debated throwing her science notebook at them.

At lunchtime, Aliya was in a particularly foul mood, not having found anyone to be on her squad. Suddenly, she heard a crash followed by a raucous burst of laughter. Dina, the self-appointed fifth-grade bully – who had spread a rumour in fourth grade that Aliya and Ahmed 'liked' each other – was laughing at Lena, a girl that Aliya recognized from her English class. Her off-white Kuwaiti scarf was covered in juice and her books were scattered all over the cafeteria floor.

Aliya couldn't pinpoint what annoyed her the most: the fact that Lena was just standing there, covered in juice, doing nothing as everyone laughed, or that Dina was pulling out her phone to take a picture. Or even that one of the books covered in juice was the one that Aliya's father had published.

Aliya was already riled up from her own frustrations and wanted to lash out. She snatched the juice box and poured its contents over Dina's head. Dina gasped as the cold liquid trickled down her face. Incensed, she screamed and ran from the cafeteria before anyone could take a picture. As Aliya felt the adrenaline fade, she knelt to help Lena pick up the rest of her stained books.

"Uhhh, thanks," Lena muttered to Aliya, pushing her glasses up the bridge of her nose.

"It's okay. She's a bully. Someone had to stand up to her," said Aliya, although she was already beginning to worry about the repercussions of this confrontation. To stop these mounting thoughts, she quickly blurted out, "Hey, do you play video games?"

"No," Lena said, "I don't really have time. My brother and I don't own any game consoles."

Of course not, Aliya thought to herself, irritated, looking at the number of books in Lena's hands, not to mention the enormous backpack hunkered over her shoulders. "Never mind."

Aliya had just turned away, when she heard Lena quietly say, "There are a few books in the library that have chapter books based on different video games."

Aliya had never been much of a reader. Her interests lay only in gaming, but perhaps spending time with Lena would help her in both. "Cool, let's get you cleaned up and then you can show me where the books are."

Lena grinned and Aliya felt the spark of a new and unexpected friendship.

CHAPTER 5

Later that day, Aliya was playing Minecraft, trying out strategies from some of the books Lena had suggested. After two hours, though, she realized that she was starving. Her mother usually cut up some fruit while she played, but she hadn't seen much of her mother all afternoon.

As she walked to her mother's room, she heard a strange sound. Aliya opened the door and was shocked to see her mother lying on the floor, crying and gasping, phone in hand.

"Mama! What happened? What is it?" Aliya tried to get her mother to sit, but she wouldn't budge. There were streaks of blood on the carpet, and Aliya saw that the bandage her father had placed carefully on her wrist a few days earlier had been ripped off. She shook her mother. "Tell me! Is it Baba? What is it?" Her mother wouldn't respond. She continued to cry and pull at her skin.

With one hand, Aliya grabbed her mother's wrist to prevent her from hurting herself. With the other, she grabbed her mother's phone and quickly tapped in the passcode to unlock it. The first thing she saw was a string of messages between her mother and Reem. Most of the messages were from her mother, growing more and more frantic with each one. Reem had placed the house on the market weeks before and sold it, all under her own name. Now she understood why her mother was distraught. She had lost one of her biggest clients and her best friend in one day.

Aliya held on to her mother, murmuring soft assurances, but nothing seemed to make a difference to her mother's state. She lay down next to her, clutching her hand tightly to prevent any more harm from occurring. As her mother fell into an uneasy silence, staring at the ceiling, Aliya had an unnerving feeling that her mother didn't even notice she was there.

Over the next few days, Aliya tried to focus on her studies. She had a big maths test coming up and she wanted to show her father that she could balance her schoolwork and gaming. Each day, however, she found herself spending more time with her mother. A dramatic change had come over Basma. She had become a shell of herself, moving from room to room, phone in hand, obsessively watching the steps of the house deal go through. Aliya tried prying the phone from her, but her mother got angry and tried to hit her.

Hurt from this encounter, Aliya went upstairs to avoid her mother's strange behaviour, but she couldn't concentrate on her work or her gaming. As the days passed, marks continued to appear on her mother's arms and wrists, sometimes in the form of scratches and sometimes actual cuts. Aliya considered taking the knives and hiding them – it's not like her mother was cooking these days anyway. Tonight's dinner, for example, was yet another meal of boxed macaroni and cheese.

"I don't know how to help her," Aliya confessed to Lena later that week.

"Hmm," Lena considered as they made their way to English class, "maybe I'll come over with my mum and they can become friends? Then, your mother will forget about what happened."

Aliya wasn't sure how meeting Salma could possibly replace a decades-old friendship with Reem, but it was worth a shot.

Later that day, when Aliya told her mother that they were having company over the weekend, her mother reacted in a way that she never expected. She got to work. Indeed, for the rest of the week, her mother cleaned up the entire house and planted a set of beautiful purple geraniums in the flower bed, and, on the night itself, prepared a delicious meal of chicken pilau and mint-yogurt chutney – Aliya's favourite dish.

When the doorbell rang, Aliya's mother smoothed over the creases of her *kurta* and quietly said, "I know I've been out of it. I got depressed over the house deal, but I'm better now. I'll talk to your dad about it when he gets back from his trip and we will all get through it together. I promise."

She winked and Aliya breathed a sigh of relief.

CHAPTER 7

After dinner, the mothers had a cup of *karak chai* while Lena and Aliya sat in the living room, doing some last-minute revision before the maths test.

"Be right back," Aliya said. "I left my calculator in the kitchen." She was about to step inside when she heard the sound of her mother crying.

"You must be thankful, Basma," Salma was saying, reassuringly. "Think of all the things you have in your life. Maybe you could pray for yourself." Aliya heard her mother cry even more.

She peered through the slightly ajar door until she could see both mothers perched on the kitchen stools, with their backs to her. Salma reached out to pat Basma's arm, but she quickly pulled away.

Salma looked around surreptitiously, not noticing Aliya, and quietly said, "There is someone you can talk to. Someone who can help you... and stop him."

Aliya's mother shot up so quickly that the stool clattered to the floor. "I think you have the wrong impression," she said. She picked up the stool and placed it firmly under the kitchen island, an indication that it was time for Salma and Lena to leave. When they did, Lena gave Aliya a puzzled look, while Aliya stared at her mother, bewildered.

Later that night, Aliya lay awake in her bed, waiting for her mother to tuck her in as she did when her father was away traveling. It was a long time before she finally gave up and closed her eyes, falling into a fitful sleep.

* * *

Though exhausted, Aliya flew through the math test with lightning speed. She couldn't believe her luck. All those extra hours studying with Lena had paid off. For the first time, Aliya felt that she had conquered something *real*, something other than a video game, and it felt great.

After school, Aliya ran into the house and asked her mother for something she had never asked for before. "Mama, I aced the maths test! Can I sleep over at Lena's house today?"

Her mother called out from upstairs. "That's great, sweetie! Go ahead. Have fun!"

Smiling, Aliya ran upstairs, grabbed some clothes and toiletries, and stuffed them into an overnight bag. She was so excited that she didn't notice the two large suitcases standing upright in the living room.

CHAPTER 8

Lena was no stranger to sleepovers. Having grown up with cousins nearby, her basement was set up as the perfect sleepover spot. Lena's parents may not allow any gaming consoles, but they did have a *massive* television with dozens of movies for the girls to choose from. Ali, Lena's six-year-old brother, tried to sneak downstairs to watch, but as soon as Lena said, "Baba…" in a warning tone, he scurried upstairs and slammed the basement door.

Lena fell asleep halfway through the movie, so Aliya got up to turn off the DVD player. She heard Salma talking to someone and realized that Ali must not have closed the door properly. She heard her say, "I'm telling you, Noor. Basma was covered in wounds."

Aliya's breath hitched. *Why are they saying such terrible things?*

She slowly crept over to the foot of the basement stairs. She could see that the door was slightly open and that Salma's shadow was moving around, as though she was pacing in circles. "Layla told me last week that she saw her at the *masjid*, doing *wudhu* alone.

There were bruises and cuts all over her arms. It's like someone had twisted and pinched her skin."

Aliya froze, not knowing what to do. Part of her wanted to go upstairs and demand that these aunties stop talking about her mother, but she also wanted to keep on listening. Even more than that, she wanted to go home.

Aliyah looked at her watch and hesitated. It was 2am. This was her first sleepover and she didn't want to jeopardize any future sleepovers by demanding that she be dropped home early.

By now, Salma had hung up the phone, turned off the hallway light and walked away. The only light visible to Aliya was the nightlight next to where Lena was sleeping.

She crawled back into bed, but she couldn't sleep. She had known for a while that her mother was intentionally hurting herself, but she didn't like the idea of anyone else knowing about it, especially not the local Muslim community. What Aliya couldn't understand, though, was why? She wracked her brain, trying to think of a reason. Was it the house deal falling through? The ruined childhood friendship? Was it because Baba was always away on business?

No, Aliya thought. *It's because of me. I'm a terrible daughter. She needs help around the house. She needs someone to cook for her. I must stay home with her. There's no one else to do it. It's okay, I can homeschool.*

Aliya considered how she would break the news to Lena that she was dropping out of school. As she looked over at the calm, sleeping face of her new friend, Aliya felt as though her heart was breaking. She turned away and buried herself under the comforter, silent tears dripping onto the pillow as she quietly wept.

In the morning, Aliya had every intention of racing out the door as soon as she woke up. However, when she passed by the kitchen, her stomach let out a low grumble. Fatima had made stacks of chocolate-chip pancakes. There were hash browns on the table and the delicious smell of halal bacon sizzling on the stove. Aliya had not eaten any proper food in days. She sat down next to Lena and dug into the delicious food while Salma quietly looked on, not commenting on the speed with which Aliya was eating.

"You know," she said, kindly, "you're welcome to eat here any time."

Aliya felt embarrassed, even though Salma gave no indication of being aware of Aliya's eavesdropping last night.

"Thank you," Aliya said. "Can you drop me home? I promised my mother that I would be home by 10am."

"Absolutely!" Salma said, while trying to keep a six-year-old Ali from dipping his chocolate-chip pancakes into a jar of Nutella.

As they drove up, Aliya was relieved to see that her mother's car was still in the driveway. She checked her watch. Based on the schedule her father had left on the refrigerator door, Aliya knew he was already on the road and should be home in the next three hours. She thanked Salma profusely and got out of the car.

The smell hit her first. She gagged as she opened the front door. The garbage bag in the kitchen had not been emptied and there was leftover pilau and yogurt sitting on the kitchen island from two days prior, when Lena and her mom had visited.

"Mama?" Aliyah called out, walking around.
No answer.

She went into the living room.

"Mama?" she asked again. There was no sign that her mother was there.

Despite the heavy overnight bag looped on her shoulder, Aliya kept moving, quickening her pace from walking to an all-out sprint as she dashed from room to room.

The kitchen.

The bathroom.

The family room.

In each room, she didn't call out her mother's name. She screamed it, as though she could somehow wake up her mother from whatever depths of depression she may have sunk to this time.

She thundered up the stairs, two at a time, and went straight to her parent's room. There was no one there. Aliya threw off the covers as though her mother was hiding underneath. She opened her mother's closet door and screamed into it. Aliya sat down on the bed and screamed into the pillow that smelled vaguely of her mother's perfume. She began to rock back and forth, talking aloud, "She's just gone for a walk. Everything is fine. I'm not home alone."

Aliya cursed herself for not having a phone like every other fifth-grader. Her parents no longer used a landline and relied entirely on their cellphones. Resigned, she went to her room to put away the overnight bag she hadn't realized she was dragging around the house. Suddenly, she stopped. On her bed was a piece of paper that was folded and propped upright. Scrawled on the top, in her mother's handwriting, was her name.

Aliya opened the card and read:

I need help. I've known this for a while and this life, this community can't give that to me. I need to figure things out for myself and I don't want you or your dad to get hurt. I love you very much. Don't settle for being a good girl. Be the best girl. Be the best friend. You already are the best daughter.

The bag fell to the floor. As tears streamed down her face, Aliya felt a wave of emotions churning inside her.

Anger. *She left? How do you abandon a ten-year old child?*

Bitterness. *What do those women know anyway?*

Frustration. *Where is Baba? Why isn't he here?*

But the deepest feeling of all that washed over her, threatening to engulf her in a tidal wave of despair was a yawning pit of sadness. It was a pain that Aliyah had never experienced. It was the pain of knowing that the one person who understood her most in the world had chosen to leave her. This was not a goodbye. It was as though she was on the phone with her mom, staying on the line no matter what, but her mother had chosen to hang up on her.

Aliya sat down on the floor, wrapped her arms around her body and started to cry, holding herself as tightly as she could. She didn't notice the bruises that were forming on her arms.

CHAPTER 10

Two hours later, Aliya woke to the sound of her father's voice. "Where are my girls?"

Aliya could hear his booming voice echo through the hallway, but she couldn't respond. She felt weak and tired, and so she kept her eyes closed, unwilling to open them to the prospect of a life without her mother around.

Her father came into the room and rushed over to pick her up. "Aliya, look at me!" he said, sounding desperate. "Where is your mother?"

Aliyah finally opened her eyes and looked at her father. She held up the letter that was still in her hands. He read the contents quickly and then pulled out his phone. They both heard a phone ring and Aliya mustered enough strength to trail behind her father as he made his way to wherever her mother's phone was.

The phone was sitting on the bedside table. He picked it up and turned it off with a click. He then walked out of the room, right past Aliya, as though she wasn't standing in front of him, half dead. He walked around the house and Aliya closed her eyes as though she could trace his steps with her mind.

The living room.

The kitchen.

The basement.

Aliya hadn't bothered to check there because she knew her mother had an aversion to tight spaces. "It's like the walls are closing around me," her mother had said every time her father had asked for it to be cleaned out. *How ironic*, Aliya thought, *that the only walls closing in were the ones that her mother had constructed in her mind. She had trapped herself in and locked Aliya out.*

As her father walked around the house, he didn't raise his voice. It was as though he expected to find his wife occupied in the kitchen or taking a shower. He came back upstairs and found Aliya in the same place he left her. Her father knelt until he was level with her face and whispered, "Aliya, where did she go?" When Aliya saw the despair on his face, she felt her lips quiver again. The tears flowed more freely as that wave of sadness threatened to undo her again.

As he pulled her into a tight embrace, Aliya suddenly let out a yelp of pain. Her father looked on quizzically as she pulled back the sleeves of her shirt and suddenly felt an overwhelming sense of deja vu. Her arms were covered in dark bruises that she had unknowingly inflicted upon herself after reading her mother's letter. She felt a deep sense of shame and meant to pull away, but her father held on, refusing to let her go. With no wife and no mother to anchor them both, he simply held her gently and, together, they wept for hours.

CHAPTER 11

In the weeks that followed, Aliya learned more about herself than she ever thought possible. Both she and her father attended therapy sessions to cope with their loss. Each session brought many tears, but they also left each session feeling lighter. Just as the bruises on Aliya's arms healed over, the gaping wound in her heart subsided, though she knew it would never truly go away.

Fifth grade felt different for Aliya. The added responsibilities of helping her father around the house left her little time to engage in gaming. Her father no longer lectured her on the importance of schoolwork. They made it a point to work together, from cooking to maintaining the house. When Aliya FaceTimed Lena every night on her new phone, she made sure that she stayed close by so that when she caught her father staring blankly at his laptop or in the place where her mother had used to eat dinner, she would give him a hug to remind him that she was still there.

A few weeks before the end of the school year, her father politely asked Salma, Lena's mother, to take Aliya to the salon for a haircut.

"You know," the stylist said, "with this length of hair, you could add a bit of colour to it."

Aliya stared at herself in the mirror. She had grown taller and thinner over the past few months. Her long, dark hair flowed down her back. When she smiled, her cheekbones jutted out slightly, similar to her mother's face.

Aliya thought of the last time she had truly seen her mother as herself and happy. It was when she had planted the purple geraniums in the front yard. When Aliya saw those flowers, they had given her a sense of hope, that perhaps the storm of depression that raged in her mother's heart had passed.

"Purple," she said.

Lena raised her eyebrow. "Really?"

Meanwhile, Salma looked ecstatic that Aliya had chosen such a bold colour.

"Yes," Aliya said, staring at herself in the mirror. "I'm sure of it."

ACKNOWLEDGEMENTS

To Amir, who hoarded multiple copies of the first children's books I ever wrote in some undisclosed location because you were so proud of my achievements and you were worried I would just give them all away. (Which I probably did). Here we are, a quarter of a century later, and though I still can't take your criticism, I will always take your credit card.

To my parents, and my sisters Jameela and Shazia Jafri. You are my foundation, my cheerleaders, and my biggest critics. You remind me to keep working and, as Dad always says, to "reach for the stars."

To my four not-so-little children: Maryam, Hamzah, Omar and Ali. It was all for you.

Thank you Rachel, Kayleigh, Jess and the entire team at Trigger Publishing and Cherish Editions for seeing my words as something worth sharing.

To my friends-like-family who have supported me in every project, every event, every class, and every book that I've initiated.

Doha crowd: Nadia, Farah, Najla, Hiba, Erum, Tasneem, Yasmin, Munira, and Roshi.

US crowd: Hemna, Huma, Nadia, Sara, Winy, Nilofur and Mohsina.

To the One who makes everything possible.

ABOUT CHERISH EDITIONS

Cherish Editions is a bespoke self-publishing service for authors of mental health, wellbeing and inspirational books.

As a division of Trigger Publishing, the UK's leading independent mental health and wellbeing publisher, we are experienced in creating and selling positive, responsible, important and inspirational books, which work to de-stigmatize the issues around mental health and improve the mental health and wellbeing of those who read our titles.

Founded by Adam Shaw, a mental health advocate, author and philanthropist, and leading psychologist Lauren Callaghan, Cherish Editions aims to publish books that provide advice, support and inspiration. We nurture our authors so that their stories can unfurl on the page, helping them to share their uplifting and moving stories.

Cherish Editions is unique in that a percentage of the profits from the sale of our books goes directly to leading mental health charity Shaw Mind, to deliver its vision to provide support for those experiencing mental ill health.

Find out more about Cherish Editions by visiting cherisheditions.com or by joining us on:

Twitter @cherisheditions

Facebook @cherisheditions

Instagram @cherisheditions

ABOUT SHAW MIND

A proportion of profits from the sale of all Trigger books go to their sister charity, Shawmind, also founded by Adam Shaw and Lauren Callaghan. The charity aims to ensure that everyone has access to mental health resources whenever they need them.

You can find out more about the work Shaw Mind do by visiting their website: shawmind.org or joining them on

Twitter @Shaw_Mind

Facebook @ShawmindUK

Instagram @Shaw_Mind